True Ghost Stories and Hauntings

True Ghost Stories & Hauntings

Chilling Stories of Poltergeists, Unexplained
Phenomenon, and Haunted Houses

Volume II

Simon B. Murik

True Ghost Stories and Hauntings
Chilling Stories of Poltergeists, Unexplained Phenomenon, and Haunted Houses

Volume II

Simon B. Murik

Published by:
Paranormal Publishing
www.ParanormalPublishing.net

ISBN: 978-0-9971185-1-3

Acknowledgements

A special thank you to all those who shared their experiences of the paranormal to make this collection of ghost stories and hauntings possible. Whether you believe in ghosts or are just curious about the other side, we sincerely hope you enjoy reading this book.

Names and places within the stories have been changed to protect the privacy of those who contributed to this book.

Contents

Introduction 9

The Old Gray Church. 11

Alone On Alpha Base 6 25

The Wrath of Rover 31

Difficult Patients 37

My Wife ... Again 45

Sorority Sister 53

Racing the Ghost. 61

On the Run 67

Ice Skating with a Ghost 73

Late Night Arcade and the Pinball Wizard 79

Grandpa's Watch 85

In the Hospital. 93

My Uncle's Hunting Knife 101

Introduction

True Ghost Stories and Hauntings, Volume II, is the second in the extremely popular series of books featuring true ghost stories and hauntings which have been collected, reviewed, and edited by Simon B. Murik. Simon is the son of a long line of mediums and sensitives originally from Eastern Europe. Many of the stories come from his own experiences while others have been contributed by family members and those who have shared their paranormal experiences with him.

If you enjoy ghost stories and reading about paranormal experiences, you will love this book. Get ready for a few chills and goosebumps as you read about haunted houses, poltergeists, and other unexplained phenomenon!

Be sure to check out Volumes I and III of *True Ghost Stories and Hauntings* as well as other offerings from Paranormal Publishing at www.paranormalpublishing.com.

BONUS

Get 3 FREE ghost stories at

www.paranormalpublishing.com/ghoststories

The Old Gray Church

The cab pulled up to the black iron gate and the driver threw it in park. Beyond the gate the 1,000-year-old Irish church loomed over its infamous cemetery like a stone overlord. The driver bristled. With one hand still on the wheel, he turned to me. "Are you sure you want to stay here, Father? Believe me when I tell you, the stories you've heard about the place are true."

I rubbed my chin and stared through the cab's window. So much grayness. The church, the sky, the tombstones. I bit my lower lip and nodded. "Yes, I'm sure. This is what I came here for."

The driver shook his head, popped open the door, and got out. I scooted over and got out, too. It was about fifty degrees out, but the bleakness of everything made it feel chillier. The cabbie had already taken my suitcase out of the trunk and I walked up to him and handed him a fifty.

"Thank you, Father," he said as he tipped his cap. He then hurried back into the cab and sped off.

I took a deep breath and let it out. I knew the stories the cabbie was talking about and I didn't take them lightly. I couldn't.

My mentor, Daniel O'Connor, was one of those stories.

I picked up the suitcase and walked up to the gate. The church's bloody reputation had made its way Boston long before Daniel had come here to investigate; he'd lasted a week and then died of sudden heart failure while exploring the basement.

And now I was here.

Whether I believed the place was haunted or not.

I pushed open the gate and walked up three stone steps to a path that stretched past the cemetery towards the church. It started to drizzle and I quickened my pace. By the time I reached the twin oak doors of the church it was pouring. I set the suitcase down, knocked, and waited.

A few moments went by before the door creaked open to show a thin, clean-shaven man wearing black slacks and a light blue button-down shirt. He held his hand out. "Father Murphy?"

I smiled and shook it. "Yes. Michael?"

"Yes, very nice to meet you." He took my suitcase and I followed him into the church.

"How was your flight in from the States?" Michael asked as he led me past a library and down a hallway lined with windows looking out at the cemetery.

"The flight was fine—a little bumpy once we got over the UK," I said.

Michael nodded, "Yes, things always get a bit choppy at that point." We walked past a dining room with a long, cherry wood table and then the entrance to what I could see was a kitchen. I looked ahead again and Michael led me to a staircase at the end of the hall.

"So the arrangements are for three days, two nights, correct?" Michael said as he stepped up the first few stairs.

"Yes, two nights. And you'll be here the entire time?"

"I will be," Michael said as the staircase winded and a white stone hallway with windows lining the wall came into view. "Except for when I go into town, I'm always here. I inherited the church over ten years ago and we've been together ever since."

Michael reached the top and a couple of seconds later I was up there with him. I chuckled as I looked down the hundred-foot hallway. "Together, huh? You sound like you're friends with the place."

Michael's face tightened a bit and he gazed out a window. "Friends, no. Partners in some way, maybe, but not friends." He tilted his head towards the hallway. "Come on, your room's down this way.

I followed him, and when he stopped outside a small bedroom I peered in to see a full-sized bed, an old ivory dresser pressed against the far wall, and a window that overlooked the cemetery. I started to walk in and Michael grabbed my arm.

"You don't have to actually stay here, you know. There's an inn less than a mile from here … a bed and breakfast, very charm—"

"Thanks. I'll be fine here," I said and tried to pull away.

Michael's hand tightened. "You need to realize that you're on your own from this point. I can tell you where things are and answer any general questions about the church's structure itself, but I can't talk about its history or—"

I looked hard into his eyes. "I appreciate that, but I paid a thousand dollars for two nights here and I know exactly where I am. Do whatever is appropriate, but please understand, I came here to get answers.

We held each other's stare for a long second and Michael removed his hand. "Very good, Father. As I said, please let me know if there's anything I can do within the guidelines."

"Thank you. I will."

Michael turned and hustled back to the stairs like he was late to catch a train.

I walked into the room. There was a small bathroom with a little white sink and a shower to my right. I set the suitcase down by the dresser. Through the window I could see that the rain had stopped but the sky was still a blanket of gray. I walked up to it and set my hand on the glass. The tombstones stretched the entire length of the church and a thick row of trees behind the cemetery pretty much blocked my view of anything else.

I tapped my fingers against the window and stared at the tombstones. Daniel had also known what he was getting into when he came here—I didn't buy that he'd died of heart failure. I'd known the man for eight years and he was as healthy as a horse; three Iron Man Triathlons, a hell of a tennis player, and a brown belt in Judo—no way his heart just gave out on him at forty-four years old.

I rubbed the side of my face. My skin was so grimy from the long day it was like it had scotch tape stuck all over it; I headed into the bathroom and splashed cold water on it. Taking a neatly folded green towel that hung on a hook next to the sink, I dried off. Feeling a little bit fresher, I put the towel back and headed downstairs. Michael was nowhere in sight as I walked down the hall towards the library and I suddenly felt very small, almost like a child whose parents had left him inside a cold mansion by himself.

I got to the library and went straight to the stacks of hardcover books lined up on the floor-to-ceiling bookcase next to the window. Tracing my finger along the alphabetical titles, I stopped when I reached a black book with gold lettering called *Ghosts of the 1,000-Year-Old Church*. I slid it off the shelf.

The cover showed a black-and-white photo of the church I was standing in.

Opening the book, I started to thumb through the pages. Chapter after chapter described the volatile past of the church. Accidental deaths, suicides, and even murder. Daniel had been fascinated with the place ever since I'd met him. When he'd touched down in Ireland he'd called me to let me know he was here and then again the next day to tell me he was going to check out the basement.

That was the last time I ever spoke with him.

A sharp knock on the open door made my heart jump. Michael stood in the doorway. "Just wanted to let you know that dinner will be ready at six o'clock sharp."

"Sounds good," I said, nodding.

Michael took a step inside. "Settling in OK?"

I closed the book and looked around the room. "Yeah; it's a fascinating place you've got here."

Michael put his hands in his pocket and walked over to me. His face had softened. "Look, I want you to know that I do understand why you're here, and as I said before, I can't answer many questions," he leaned in a bit, "but I *can* offer you a bit of advice. Although I'm sure you're already planning on it, don't go into the basement."

I set the book back on the shelf and looked at him. "You said dinner's at six, right?"

Michael stared hard at me, but I didn't think it was to intimidate—more like he was trying to show me just how serious he was. There was a hint of fear in his eyes. His face then relaxed. He nodded, "Correct. Six." Michael turned and walked out of the library. I then headed back to my room to take a nap.

I woke up an hour and a half later and looked over at the window to see a starless black sky. Pushing myself out of bed, I stretched my arms out and went downstairs to the dining room. Michael was already seated. Sitting in the middle of the table was a thick slab of roast beef, a loaf of fresh-baked bread, and a bottle of red wine.

"Hey, Michael," I said as I walked to my chair. He didn't answer and I saw that his eyes were closed and he was mumbling to himself. "Michael," I repeated. His eyes opened and for a second he stared at me like he didn't know who I was. I sat down and reached for the wine. "You OK?" I asked.

Michael nodded, his eyes lost their blankness, and he smiled. "Yes, yes. That's a fantastic merlot. Please, enjoy it. We have a collection of over two hundred bottles."

I poured myself a glass and for the next hour Michael and I made pleasant small talk but the hidden tension was there. He knew I hadn't come all the way from Boston just to leave without answers and I knew that the fear in his eyes was real.

When I finished eating I went back into the library. Michael had started a fire in the fireplace and I flipped on the lamp next to the couch. I'd taken *Ghosts of the 1,000-Year-Old Church* from the shelf again and sat down in front of the fire with an eight-year-old bottle of Cognac that Michael had brought out for me. I took a sip and started reading.

In the first chapter, the book talked about Martin Halligan, a "dark priest" who had run the church 800 years ago. Martin had two passions: painting and killing. And by the time the town had caught on to what he was up to, he had murdered thirteen people over a span of seven years. Halligan was arrested, tried, and hung all on the same day.

The church's legacy of ghostly deaths began shortly after that.

For the next few hours I continued to read about the church's deranged history. When my eyes got heavy, I closed the book, leaned back against the couch's thick cushion, and felt myself doze off. While asleep, I dreamt that a black dragon was breathing against my face. The breath grew hotter and hotter until my skin was burning. The breath then turned ice cold.

I woke up in a dark room.

The fire had gone out and the lamp had been turned off. I got up and walked out of the room. Except for the moonlight shining through the windows, the church was dark. My watch said 1:17 a.m. and I assumed that Michael had put out the fire and gone to bed. I made my way to the staircase and went up it.

A thin, blurry man stood at the end of the hallway.

"Michael?" I called out.

He didn't answer.

I started to walk down the hall and he turned and walked into what I guessed was another bedroom. I kept going and when I reached the room I stared into total darkness.

"Michael?" I asked again.

A flash of lightning lit up the room and I saw a bunch of crucifixes hanging on the wall, a bed broken in half, and what looked like a dead white cat laying upside-down in the corner by the window.

But no one was in there.

I hurried back to my room and locked the door.

Somehow I fell asleep within the next hour and the next thing I knew it was morning.

After showering and getting dressed I went downstairs to find Michael reading the newspaper.

"Good morning, Jon. There's coffee in the kitchen," he said without looking up.

I went into the kitchen, poured a cup, and then went back out to the dining room. "Michael, did you sleep upstairs last night?"

Michael put down his paper and shook his head. "No, I never sleep upstairs."

I scratched the back of my head, "Well, it's just that I thought I saw someone standing at the end of the hall late last night and—"

"Jonathan," Michael interrupted, "Remember what I told you, I can't answer questions or discuss things like that. Whatever you saw is for you and you only."

I bit my lip and nodded. After breakfast I went back upstairs and walked down the hall to the room.

The door was closed.

I turned the handle and opened it. Nothing—completely empty. No crucifixes, no broken bed, no upside-down cat. Just plain white walls and a window. I shook my head, closed the door, and walked back down the hall. When I got back downstairs I saw a note taped to the front door of the church and went up to it.

Had to go into town. Be back soon.

- Michael

I took the note off the door and scrunched it up. This was interesting. I liked the idea of exploring the church and its grounds without Michael around.

The next couple of hours flowed by like a hazy dream. Voices whispered down the hallways, I swore I saw reflections of blurred faces in the mirrors and windows, and when I returned after wandering through the cemetery - many of the names on the tombstones matched those in the book - a fog had wrapped around the church so thick that it took me almost twenty minutes to find the big double doors again.

And then there was the basement. I'd read in the book that the entrance to it was in a hallway that ran behind between the church's nave and with Michael still gone, I figured now was as good a time as any to go down there. I walked through the kitchen and into a white-walled hallway. The entrance to the nave was across the hall just to my left and there was a door at the far end of the hallway. I went up to it and stared at its gold handle.

Time to go down there.

I opened the door.

Wooden stairs descended into candlelit darkness. I put my foot on the first step and it creaked like an old man's spine. I left the door open and started walking down. The staircase curved a bit and I counted another tens steps before I reached a cement floor. Bottles of wine lined the wall on my left side and a couple of candles flickered on the wall to my right. Had Michael come down here and lit them for me?

My gut said no.

Straight ahead more candles illuminated a white stone hallway that looked like it stretched out at least two hundred feet from the room I was in.

And then I looked up and my stomach twisted like I'd just drank a bottle of turpentine.

A mural of death covered the ceiling. Priests slitting their own throats, strangling each other, hanging themselves—one with a narrow face and long, black hair was clutching his heart, his face twisted in pain.

Daniel.

I bit my lip and looked ahead. Somehow I knew the answer to what happened to Daniel was down that hall.

I walked forward. The hallway was similar to upstairs: cold and impersonal. I thought about Michael's warning.

But I kept going.

A black cloud crept out of the ceiling.

I stopped and watched as it swirled towards me. It was almost as wide as the hall and my heart suddenly felt like it had a syringe filled with misery stuck in it. I took a step back and felt hot breath on my face.

And then it was ice cold.

Everything went dark.

I turned around and started to run back down the hall but the hallway seemed to curve and swerve in the darkness and I smacked into the wall. My forehead ached and I couldn't get a bearing on which way was which. A cold sweat broke out on my body and my heart raced. I stumbled ahead not knowing if I was heading back towards the mural room or straight at that cloud.

And then in the darkness I saw a thin, pale face and the white collar of a priest's vestment under it floating towards me.

"Daniel?" I whispered.

It said nothing and as it came closer.

I let out a weeping chuckle as the pain and sadness of everyone who'd come here before me smothered my body and soul. My chest squeezed tight and I struggled to breathe.

A hand grabbed my forearm like an iron vise and pulled me away. "I told you not to come down here, Father!" Michael's voice snapped. He dragged me through the blackness and seconds later we were back in the dimly lit mural room. Michael pulled me to the stairs and I ran up them and into the church hallway. I collapsed onto the floor. Breathing hard, Michael started dragging me by my arm down the hallway. "It won't come upstairs but we shouldn't stay this close." After about twenty feet he let go and I slumped to the floor; Michael sat down next to me with his back against the wall.

"So did you get your answers?" he asked.

My head had stopped spinning and my chest had relaxed. "Almost," I said. I looked over at the thin man. "Who are you, Michael?"

Michael rubbed his hands together and looked at the floor. "In the book about the church's history you read about the dark priest, correct?"

I pushed myself to my elbows.

"Well, what the book doesn't tell you is that just before he'd been hung, this dark priest set a curse on the church. And that after his death, anyone who went into the basement and viewed his mural would be haunted by its ghosts." Michael looked at me. "This way, under a stream of caretakers that Martin could trust, the mural could be continued."

I bit down on my lower lip and then let it go. "Caretakers who Martin could trust—caretakers who shared his bloodline," I pieced together.

Michael stared hard at me. "That's right. I am Michael Walker Halligan. And it's been very nice to meet you, Father."

I lay back down, stared at the ceiling, and chuckled.

Alone On Alpha Base 6

The moon's gray rock floor sprawled into the black horizon. I tapped the hallway-length window with my fingers and sighed. Six months I'd been up here on Alpha Base 6. Why they'd tacked the 6 on the end I had no idea; there was only one base on this cold rock, just like there was only one person—me.

But it's not like I didn't know what I was getting into.

My friends had said I was out of my mind to take a two-year stint up here and they might have been right. The guy before me had been killed performing observational experiments on some crater about six miles from the base and I'd be lucky not to suffer at least some level of radiation poisoning by the time I got off of here.

But a half-million bucks for the gig was worth it.

I cracked my knuckles and walked down the steel hallway into my quarters. A junior-sized bed, small desk, and a nice view of the north side of the moon was about all it had going for it. Yawning, I walked over to the bed. I'd been working since 0600 and needed a quick nap or I was liable to wander outside without my helmet on. I lay down, closed my eyes, and a cold breeze suddenly flowed over my face.

My eyes popped back open.

A thin white blur hovered in the center of the room. I shut my eyes and opened them again. It was gone.

"This damn place," I said as I turned over and went to sleep.

Three hours later I was up and back at work. The roaming satellite had spotted a nice patch of golden ore just a couple of miles away and I wanted to mark the location and send it to the company to get the OK to dig. I began to take down the coordinates when another cold breeze hit my back.

I turned around and my heart froze.

A pair of blurry white hands gripped the inside of the doorway like they were struggling to keep an unseen body from flying away. The hands let go and I got out of my chair and went into the hallway.

Nothing.

I rubbed my temples and then checked my pulse. Jesus, I was barely a quarter of a way through this job and I was already seeing things.

I headed to the communications center to transfer the data about the ore and get the go-ahead to extract it. When I got there I punched the coordinates into the computer and hit send. It would be a few minutes until I got a response and I leaned back in the chair and closed my eyes. When I opened them up a few seconds later the computer screen was white static. I stood up and looked around the room; the three other computer screens were also all static. It could have been a solar block, but that was unlikely. Putting my hands on my hips, I bit my lower lip and stared at the floor for a second.

Was five hundred grand worth it?

I shook my head and looked back up. The screens were back to normal.

A message came through and I was cleared to get the ore. As soon as I stepped back into the hallway, a noise like a wrench banging against a metal pipe rang through the station and the back of my neck got tight. It sounded like it'd come from the west end of the base and I ran down the hall, made a right, and then a quick left to see the Records Room's white fluorescent light on. A thick, wavy white figure—almost like a blurry space suit—stepped out of the light and into the doorway. It disappeared back into the light as fast as it had emerged and when I got to the room nothing was there.

No doubt about it, I was cracking up.

And yet …

The company had barely given me any information about my predecessor's death. The report I'd received had just said there'd been an accident resulting in the death of an employee while performing a lunar experiment and what was called a Quick Crew had come and retrieved the body before I'd arrived. The exact location of the site where he'd died had not been given and the files that had the info were locked in the computer as "Top Secret."

I entered the Records Room and naturally it was empty. However, the company's silver logo floated across the screen of the computer. At the bottom of the screen were the words "Access Granted."

I went to the computer and clicked the mouse. The logo disappeared and a three-dimensional overview of a path from the base to a location with a green laser beacon marked "Crater" appeared.

Top secret or not, I was going to go take a look at the site for myself.

I hurried to the changing room next to the air lock, put my moon suit on, and then walked into the air lock and hit the "Open Portal" button on the wall. There was a mechanical grumble and the two metal halves of the circular door began to slide away from each other. Ten seconds later the portal was clear.

I stepped through it. The rover was parked next to a big gray boulder about thirty feet away from the portal and I walked over to it. Grabbing the two handlebars outside of the rover's door, I pulled myself up, opened the door, and slid in. It was the first time I'd been in the rover in a few days and it felt good to be outside the base. I flipped the ignition switch and the dashboard and headlights lit up. Pressing down on the accelerator I gripped the thick steering wheel and accelerated forward.

For the next fifteen minutes I rumbled over rocks and up and down small hills towards the site. When I saw the beacon I pulled the rover up to it, climbed out, and walked over to the edge of the crater. It was about a hundred feet deep and maybe a mile wide.

At the bottom I could see a body.

I carefully sidestepped down the crater and over to the body. The nameplate on the suit said "Walker." Kneeling down, I ran my hands over the suit and inspected the golden visor. No tears or cracks.

Whatever had killed him had been internal.

And the company had never actually come to get him or even give him a burial.

Loneliness sunk through me like a stone sinking in the ocean and I looked to the west. At the top of the crater a blurry white figure stood at the edge looking down at me. We stared at each other for a few seconds and then it seemed to just drift into the darkness and moon rock.

I nodded, stood up, and made my way back up the crater to the rover. When I got there I hopped inside and started driving back across the lunar desert to the base. I didn't know what had happened to Walker and I'd probably never find out. But I'd return to bury him.

Because five hundred grand might have covered me cracking up, but it didn't cover being haunted by a dead astronaut's ghost while alone on Alpha Base 6.

The Wrath of Rover

I killed my dog when I was six.

She was a Maltese puppy, hardly bigger than a good-sized hamster when I killed her. It wasn't an accident. It was childhood sadism, a mean streak that ther0apists claimed they'd managed to remove shortly after the death of the tiny pooch.

I don't even remember her name any more, probably one of those dumb dog names small kids come up with, like Spot or Rover. I remember I thought she was a male for the first few months we owned her.

I hardly remember the deed, honestly. We were playing fetch with a stick, and I started to throw the stick at her. The next thing I knew, the sticks became rocks and my pet wasn't playing anymore. Just whimpering. Then … not.

My parents sent me to a therapist, and the therapist told me to value life and become a hippie or a vegetarian or something. I wasn't really paying attention. I did feel bad about my once-pet, though, and told my parents that I didn't want to have another animal. It didn't take too much convincing. I avoided animals for years after that, and they made it really easy to avoid me. When they saw me coming they would step back, stay away from me. I guess maybe they could smell what I'd done. I'd heard crazy stories about that sort of thing, dogs smelling guilt and earthquakes, like they have some sort of sixth sense.

I did eventually become a vegetarian—for health reasons, not because I valued the lives of the cattle. I had some gastro-intestinal issues that the doctors told me about without using a single word that I actually knew the meaning of.

One day, after school, as I was walking home, I noticed cats jumping in fear and running away when they saw me. I stepped on an anthill, but none of the insects bit me—they just ran away. I came into my home, our neighbor's goat bleating and kicking at her fence, and told Genevieve to please shut up.

Why did our neighbors have a goat!? Eventually Genevieve bleated herself out and was quiet, so I could get started on my homework. In biology we'd started studying mice. My class had to fill out research papers at home while we took care of mice in class. Oh, yeah. That was going to work out just fine.

It did not work out just fine. Adorable little Penrose, a little white mouse who wouldn't hurt a fly, jumped into our teacher's beard and frantically began biting in a blind panic. The projects were cancelled, videos were leaked, and the entire situation was mess. But biology is a high school requirement, because I totally have a career ahead of me studying animals. On the plus side, Dr. Hayka had a project planned to replace the cancelled mouse study very quickly: mouse dissections.

Dead animals hardly ever run away.

In that vein, some kid thought it was a great idea to bring her pet snake into lunch to show it off. It wasn't venomous, or ten students would be dead right now, so I guess there's that. This did not, however, stop the hefty lawsuits, investigations, and rather annoying snake hunt that involved me standing in the hallway to stop the snake from entering the cafeteria. I was there for nearly an hour, being scary to a snake that wouldn't show up.

This was a standard day, aside from the arrival of the serpent. Animals shun me, panic when forced to be near me. That's why it was such a shift when they stopped.

Maybe everyone else was living like this the whole time, but not being feared by animals is just awful. I hadn't been bitten by ants in my entire living memory; now they sought me out. I found that I hated the red monsters; I hated their burning bite. Cats would hiss and scratch at me, and dogs … *dogs*. It was as though they had a personal vendetta against me, as if they somehow knew that I had killed one of their own. I heard barking all night, complemented by Genevieve's angry bleating. The entire animal kingdom seemed to have been mobilized in a war against me.

Every day during in the summer, I would wake up with mosquito bites on my face.

Genevieve tried to bite me as I walked by her fence, pushing against the painted wood. She bleated angrily at me, almost as if she were saying *come back and fight, you yellow-bellied murderer!*

I had no idea where the words came from. I'd certainly never thought of anything that strange. But when I stopped to think about it, I was stung by a wasp.

Animals are monsters. They are vicious, powerful creatures and I am sure that they would gladly tear me apart and feast on my remains. Almost all of them have mouths and can bite, and they will bite given any—or, more often, no—provocation.

For weeks the hells that suburban nature could unleash dogged me. Bites, stings, scratches, and howls of rage followed me from every corner. I lived in constant fear of the lower level of the food chain. I felt that I could never be more afraid when my dog spoke to me when I fell asleep one night outside on the hammock.

I assume that if a dog spoke to anyone they would be shocked. The fact that she was dead didn't make it much more plausible. And yet the pooch I knew from childhood appeared to me, in perfect health, just as alive as she'd been the day before I'd brutally killed her.

"Well, well, well. You're looking awful. It's like someone *viciously stoned you to death*," she said bitterly.

I didn't say anything for a while, but when I found my voice I stuttered out an apology.

"I am so sorry, Rover."

So I had named her Rover. That was a good thing to know.

"I was only a child," I tried to explain.

Rover barked at me in a way that made by blood curdle.

And just then Genevieve hopped the fence and was heading full speed towards me. Within a split second, she knocked me off the hammock and onto the ground. I was under her kicking hooves. A sharp blow hit my head.

Darkness.

Difficult Patients

shot out of bed, slid the nightstand drawer open, and grabbed my gun. The thumping noise had come from the weight room down the hall and it was the third night in a row I'd heard it. I tapped the sensor on the wall and the hallway and exercise room lit up. I held the gun out and walked down the hall into the room.

Nothing.

The rack of dumbbells was organized, the medicine balls were neatly stacked, and the bench press had two forty-five pound plates on each side. Exactly how I'd left it.

But I was positive I'd heard a heavy thud repeatedly hit the black, matted floor.

Three nights in a row this had happened and four nights ago was when Johnny had died from a gut shot wound on my operating table—the one that I used in my office to moonlight for our local crime family

Difficult patients. Awful people.

But did they ever pay well.

Johnny was a superstitious guy though and wound up really tight. I'd gotten the call at 1:17 a.m. that he'd gotten plugged by a rival mob guy and he needed immediate fixing. Twenty-five grand in cash on the spot. Who wouldn't mind dealing with these assholes for that? But the damage was too vicious and I'd lost him while he was underneath.

And now I was hearing noises late at night.

I spent the rest of the night watching TV and the next morning did fifty laps in the pool, showered, and then went out to Joey's Omelets for breakfast. It was just after ten when I got to Joey's and I took a table next to the window. Angela, the waitress, saw me as she poured a fat guy with receding gray hair some coffee and nodded. Five minutes later she set down my usual Greek omelet and tall glass of orange juice.

As I ate the omelet and sipped orange juice I thought about the mess I'd gotten myself into. God damn Johnny Corsico. I had the busiest practice in town and I'd graduated third in my class in med school.

But Johnny hadn't cared about any of that. In fact, other than money, women, and guns, Johnny hadn't cared much about anything. I couldn't even remember how I'd gotten hooked up with the family anymore, but after seven years of dealing with them the money barely made it worth it.

And now, thanks to Johnny buying it on the operating table, I couldn't sleep through the night.

Twenty minutes later Angela brought the bill and hurried off to seat a chattering group of tennis-playing house wives who'd just walked in. I set a twenty on the bill, got up, and pushed my chair in. The bill blew off the table onto the gray, carpeted floor and I picked it up and put it back on. The slight breeze from the ceiling fan didn't seem strong enough to blow the bill off the table, but who the hell knew? I picked the money up and put it back on the table. I started to turn and the corner of my eye caught the bill blowing off the table again. I shook my head and looked at. Picking it up again, I put it on the table and slapped the empty glass over it. The bill stayed still.

I really needed a vacation.

Southern Utah was supposed to be nice this time of year.

I spent the rest of the afternoon with Jane, my administrator, at the practice. At 3:30 my cell phone rang. It was Vince, Johnny's brother. This wouldn't be fun. Vince questioned me over what happened to Johnny like a pit bull that'd just learned to speak English. I explained that the bullet had ruptured Johnny's internal organs and nothing could be done. Vince hung up and so did I.

I looked at Jane and told her she could take off for the weekend. She grabbed her coat and left and I started to check over some paperwork when a high-pitched sound came out of the break room down the hall. I hurried to the break room and saw an empty coffee pot sizzling on the coffee maker. I turned the coffee maker off and took off the pot. Black burn marks covered the bottom of the glass and I ran it under cold water. Smoke flared from the pot and when it died out I set it in the sink. It was really hard to imagine Jane leaving the pot on the coffee maker like that, but as out of it as I'd been for all I knew I could have done it myself.

My phone rang again and I took it out of my pocket and looked at the screen. It was Johnny's number. I watched the number blink as the phone rang and after a few seconds the voice mail light went on. About twenty seconds later the light went off. I hit play on the voice mail and a blur of static twisted into my ear. I hung up and deleted it.

I'd worked seventy hours this past week and that included the Johnny thing. I didn't want to deal with any of these guys anymore and it wasn't like any of them really had anything on me to force me to keep being their after-hours doc.

But these weren't easy people to walk away from.

I closed down the office and drove home. I was meeting Star, my semi-girlfriend for dinner tonight and I wanted to get a workout in and shower up. I got home and when I walked in the house it was like I'd stepped into a sauna. I checked the thermostat but the AC was at its usual sixty-seven degrees. My skin suddenly felt cooler and I could feel the cool breeze from the vent on the wall above me. Just tired and stressed, I guessed. I got my workout in and then swam for a bit before hitting the shower.

That night at dinner, I couldn't focus and my eyes kept shifting. Johnny's guys knew this place. They came here a couple of times a month to blow off steam and although I didn't recognize any faces, there were enough sharkskin suits to make me nervous. The waiter came and I ordered a Jack and coke. A minute later the waiter returned with it and I took a sip and looked around the restaurant. When I looked back half the drink was gone.

"Did you take a drink of that?" I asked Star.

She stared at me with her big green eyes like I'd started juggling the silverware. "No, Michael, you did."

I was pretty sure I hadn't.

"Did you see me take a drink?" I asked.

"I don't know," she said flipping her hand in the air, "I wasn't really watching. But who in the hell else would have?" Star picked up her glass of wine and slightly shook her head as she took a sip.

I rubbed the side of my face. "I'm going to go to the bar for a second, do you want anything?" I asked.

She shook her head and I got up and walked to the sleek black bar at the front of the restaurant. The stools were all taken by men in thousand-dollar suits and their leggy dates. I walked up behind a guy in a tan suit and his date, who was wearing a shiny silver dress.

As I watched the bartender mixing drinks, a thick-necked guy sidled up to me. I could see in the corner of my eye that his black suit wrapped around his powerful frame like a scuba suit and he reeked of cologne. "Don't make me ever hear your voice mail again," a rough voice said.

"Look, pal," I said, turning to him. There was no one there; all I saw was a waiter scurry by and a couple of twenty-something girls in black dresses giggling over their phone a few feet away. I rubbed my forehead. *Now I'm having conversations with guys who aren't there.*

"What can I get you, sir?" an eager voice asked. I turned back to the bar. "Jack and Coke." The bartender nodded and hurried off. A minute later I had the drink and walked back to my table.

I numbly made it through the rest of the dinner. I knew the men in sharkskin suits were watching me and my food tasted as flat as cardboard.

I took Star home and she jumped out of the car. "I'll call you," I said.

"Don't bother," she snapped.

"Perfect," I said and drove off.

I turned on the radio—static. I flipped the dial around and it was just static station after static station. I smacked the wheel as my racing mind swore it heard "Die ... you let me die," scratch out of the static.

I imagined south Utah had little to no gangster activity.

I got home, sat in the Jacuzzi for an hour, and then went to bed.

The nightly thump rocked me out of my sleep and I rushed into the exercise room.

Nothing.

Screw it.

I went to my computer and typed in Moab, Utah. Images of red desert canyons and clean, blue sky came up. I booked a flight.

A month later I was looking over the Canyonlands in Moab from the patio of the condo I'd rented. I had plenty of money and had paid for everything in cash, sold the practice by proxy, and didn't tell a soul about the move. Most of my stress was gone and there were no more thumps in the night.

Had Johnny's pissed off ghost really been harassing me or had it all just been in my stressed-out mind?

Who knew.

But there were no more gangsters and I'd gotten a fresh start. And that was more than many people get in one life.

My Wife ... Again

I t's been six weeks since I buried my wife of over fifty years and I still can't get along too well without her in my life. Betty was my life and soul and I'm lost without her. We knew each other since my family moved into her neighborhood when I was six. We were boyfriend and girlfriend in high school and yes, I married my high school sweetheart, a marriage everyone told us wouldn't last. I don't know how I could have lived without her. A better match could only be found in heaven. Now I spend the better part of the day wandering around my house hoping to see my wife walk by. I know she's gone, but I have had a hard time accepting that I'll never see her again.

Everything in the house reminds me of her. The collection of figurines on the fireplace mantel, the pots and pans I cook with, the his-and-her towels in the bathroom, pictures on the wall, and pretty much everything else in the house. It's overwhelming at times; I thought of getting rid of her things or moving to another house, but the idea of doing that caused me more grief than by being reminded of her in the house we shared and loved.

Shortly after the funeral, I began to see things; I thought I was on the verge of a mental breakdown. For example, one day I was wandering around the house trying to figure out what I was going to do—that was when I thought I'd have to get rid of her things. I kept a photograph of her on my dresser and that was one of the first things I saw every morning when I got up. It was hard to look at the lovely picture of her when she was young and beautiful and life was fresh and new for us. It hurt me to see it and I turned it around so I wouldn't be faced with it every day. I thought I'd only do it until I could come to terms with her being gone.

I woke up one morning and as I went to the bathroom I stopped in surprise. The picture was facing out again and I could see her sweet face. I thought it was strange and wondered if I'd somehow turned it around and didn't remember doing it. Without much thought, I turned it back around and took care of my morning business. As I came back into my room, the picture was turned around again. A chill went through me and I couldn't do anything but stare at it for a few minutes before I turned it back around. I kept an eye on it for a few minutes, getting the weirdest feeling, as if a low-level electrical charge was running through me. It made me shudder and the hairs on my arm actually stood up and tingled.

Not much happened for the next few days, but then another strange incident occurred. While making dinner, one of the boxes of pasta I kept in the cupboard fell out onto the counter. I didn't feel any kind of movement or earthquake or anything like that, and I just stood there staring at the box. As I looked, feeling a little bit strange about it, I noticed it was my wife's favorite kind of pasta. I walked over and put it back in the cupboard, making sure the cupboard door was closed. To be honest I don't remember if it was closed or not when I came in, but out of habit I had always closed them so it left me perplexed. Even still, it wasn't normal and I felt myself again shuddering at the thought of it. The house no longer felt the same; it felt like there was a presence here. It was odd and uncomfortable.

Later that evening when I was watching television and nodding off in my chair, the channel on the TV changed and startled me. The remote was on the table and I know I hadn't touched it and I really began to feel worried. I didn't know what was happening and being alone, and rather advanced in age, I began to wonder about my sanity or if I was doing things I was unaware of. I was sitting in the chair thinking about this when I noticed the show that was on was one of my wife's favorite shows she had watched religiously. I wasn't too fond of it; if I had changed the channel, why I would have changed it to this?

Was my subconscious making me do things to remind me of my wife? I'd heard of some pretty interesting things that grieving people did and I thought maybe I was doing that too. Didn't seem like it to me though; I was old but not senile. I flicked off the TV and headed to bed. Wouldn't you know it? That damn picture was turned around facing me again! Now I really began to get spooked. This time I turned it around and laid it down so the picture was facing the dresser.

My sleep was restless and I didn't sleep well, almost jumping at every little sound the house made. Sounds I'd heard for years but now I couldn't help but wonder if someone was in the house trying to drive me crazy. I must have finally dozed off and when I woke up, the first thing I did was look at that picture. It was standing up facing me—now I began to panic.

What the hell was going on? I thought that I must be dreaming all this; this kind of stuff isn't real. I tried to ignore what was going on because I didn't believe in these types of things which I refer to as goofy crap. I decided to just ignore it all and pretend I didn't see any of this. That didn't work.

I'd spent the last week not responding to anything; I didn't turn the picture back around or even try to figure out any of the other odd things, like the box of pasta, going on during that week. Then something happened that set me to trembling. I headed to bed that night and the picture was turned so it faced the door, almost like she was looking at me. That was it; I'd had enough. I left the house and got a hotel room just to get away for a night and try to figure this stuff out. I have to admit, I was scared.

I realized I couldn't ignore this anymore; whatever it was that was happening was real and I had to accept that. What I hadn't counted on was being afraid to go back to my house. I didn't understand any of this but I did realize that something was happening that I couldn't put words to. When I woke up the next morning I just sat on the bed trying to get the courage up to go home. I couldn't and paid for another night. This was just scaring the hell out of me and I didn't know what I should do. I thought of calling my son but we weren't real close and I'm sure he would have thought I was losing my mind so I didn't. That night I had nightmares involving Betty and I woke up terrified.

They were not real, of course, but all I could remember was her calling out for me and I couldn't reach her and then she disappeared with a look of sadness on her face. I decided to go back home no matter what I felt and if it got real bad, I'd seek professional help. Maybe they had an answer for what I was going through, although I didn't think that they would. I pulled up in my driveway and couldn't get out of the car; I was actually trembling at the thought of what I'd see in the house. I felt foolish for being so afraid and before I could talk myself out of it and head back to the hotel, I grabbed my bag and headed in.

When I opened the front door and looked in, I dropped my bag and just stared. I could feel that someone was in there and I felt that weird electrical charge again. I began to shiver and I looked around. There were fresh-cut flowers on the mantle. Soft music, music my wife loved, played softly in the background and when I went in, I could smell the perfume I always liked her to wear. I was either going crazy or something else was going on—my wife was here in spirit. I found my heart racing and I started sweating in fear when I moved further into the house. The presence felt even stronger.

I walked slowly into my bedroom and not only found the picture of her on my dresser, but another of the both of us after we'd been married for about fifteen years. While I stared at the pictures, a voice right next to my ear said my name, "Ezra." I jumped and spun around but there was nothing there. The voice had sounded hauntingly like my wife's and I got goosebumps when I heard it. I sat down on my bed and gave up. I gave in to the feeling of her being all around me and actually spoke to her.

"Betty, is that you?"

My words fell on quiet and I wondered what was going on with me when I heard her voice saying my name in my ear again. I looked around and asked, "Honey, where are you?" I was trembling and didn't know if it was in anticipation or I was just scared to death.

Again I waited and nothing happened for about three minutes. Then, I saw a shimmering form start to materialize in front of me by the door. It was her! I'll be damned, it was my lovely wife! I felt at peace as I watched her glide closer to me and my heart raced, thumping loudly in my chest.

She smiled at me and leaned over to speak in my ear. "I will always love you. Be well, my love, and we will be together again soon."

With that said, she was gone. I guess she just wanted to say goodbye because after that, none of the weird stuff ever happened again. I was at peace and no longer afraid of dying—my Betty had showed me that. I was happier and I now knew that the ghosts of loved ones were always around you. You may not know it, but I guarantee you they are.

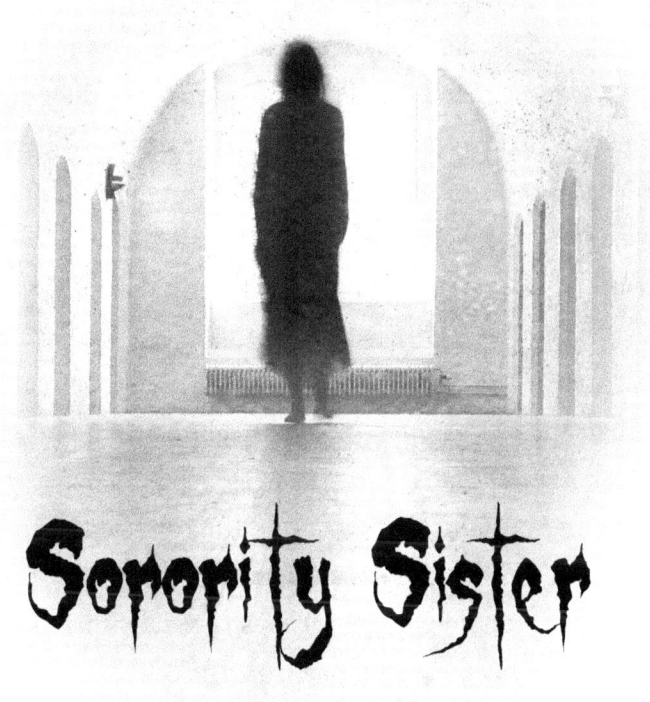

Sorority Sister

As Heather swung the Jeep up the hill she shot me a smile. "So look, the night isn't easy but you make it through and you're an Alpha Delta."

I nodded and stared ahead. The late evening sun hit the mid-October red and orange leaves so strongly they made the tree branches look like they were on fire. The dirt road curved left and I saw the cabin. It looked like it was built from perfectly smooth Red Cedar wood with a bright and clean rectangular window and a charming little cobblestone porch. The wind blew some dry leaves across the porch and it felt like we were in some secluded forest resort area a hundred miles away from school—in reality, we were less than three. I gripped my smart phone tight and checked the weather, it was supposed to rain in a couple hours.

Heather brought the Jeep up to the front of the cabin and put it in park. I wasn't scared, ghosts had never been my thing, but the idea of being out here by myself wasn't exactly thrilling.

I grabbed my overnight bag from the back seat. "So the place is really haunted by some dead family?" I asked.

Heather looked at the cabin, took a deep breath, and exhaled. She turned to me with a tight face. "Just stay out of the bedroom and you'll be fine. OK?"

A little dramatic but whatever. "OK," I said.

Heather smiled again. "See you at 9:00 a.m. tomorrow, Amy."

I hopped out of the Jeep and Heather backed out and sped off. I looked at the cabin. Maybe I wouldn't even go in. I could just sit on the porch and wait it out until morning. But that would be admitting that I was scared and I wasn't about to do that. It was going to rain tonight anyways.

I walked up the steps to the patio and looked back at the road. The sun had set and the fiery fall colors had dulled. I turned the doorknob and walked in.

The cabin was dark but I saw a switch right next to me on the wall and flipped it on. Two spearmint-green lamps at opposite corners of a sort of living room lit up. It was actually pretty nice. Clean wall-to-wall beige carpet covered the floor and a cushy, amber-colored recliner sat next to the window. The walls were smoothly painted white, and on the far wall framed photos hung of what looked like a smiling and laughing family doing various activities. Across the room and just to the right of the photos was a room with two full-sized beds; next to it was a small bathroom with a porcelain gray sink and toilet. Straight across from me was a small kitchen with a silver sink, a white stove, and a round plastic table for four.

I set my bag down and walked over to the bedroom. It was darker in here, no windows, and the air was thick like a musty attic that no one ever visited. The beds were made so tight with black and red comforters that they looked like a kind of skin around the beds. I closed the door. Like Heather had told me to, I'd be staying out of here.

The wind howled outside and I sat down, took my laptop out of my bag, and started watching a detective show on Netflix. After a couple of hours I started to doze off.

I woke up with my heart racing to the sound of a door rattling. The cabin door wasn't moving at all and just as I turned to check the bedroom door, the noise stopped. I got up and walked into the bathroom. Turning the sink on I splashed warm water on my face and then patted my face dry with a crimson towel that hung on a metal rack across from the sink. My racing heart slowed down and I went back out into the living room. Glancing over at the photo wall, I noticed a few of the photos were tilted—were they like this before and I just hadn't noticed? I didn't know, but my heart started to beat a little faster again. Walking up to the photos, I quickly straightened them and then looked at the bedroom door. I could swear it'd been rattling but maybe it had just part of a dream I was having.

I checked my watch. It was 11:27 p.m.

I looked over at the window but all I could see was the black night. Walking over to the window, I put my fingertips on the glass and a flash of lighting lit up the road and the woods in bright white light. An instant later everything went dark again with the soft thud of big rain drops starting to hit the roof of the cabin.

I went to my overnight bag, unzipped it, and took out the pint-sized bottle of black cherry vodka I'd brought. I wasn't much of a drinker but the girls had suggested I bring it just in case I needed help making it through the night. I twisted the cap off and took a sip.

A little harsh on my throat but not bad.

I sat back down and started watching some movie about high school girls being mean to each other. I took another sip of vodka and my back muscles relaxed; after about twenty minutes my eyes got heavy and started to close. They popped back open when the door started rattling again. It sounded like someone trying to open a door without turning the handle.

The instant I started to turn my head to the door the noise stopped.

When I did see the door it was perfectly still.

I took a deeper sip of the vodka and with the bottle in my hand walked back over to the wall of photos. This time I studied the pictures more closely and suddenly the happy smiling faces of the children suddenly didn't seem so happy. The grins on their faces looked strained, like they were being forced open by invisible hooks and the warm parental smiles of the mother and father now seemed more like the tight lipped smirks of a couple of snakes sneaking up an unsuspecting bunny rabbit. Photo after photo was like this. In each one the kids were staring into the camera while the parents stared at the kids: at the playground, walking through the woods, shopping in town ... The last picture was a family photo of all of them standing in the bedroom.

There was no way I was going back to sleep and it was only 12:43 a.m. I stepped away from the photos and went back to the window. The rain had stopped and the moon faintly glowed through the black clouds like a big white light bulb covered in thick gauze.

In the window's reflection the space under the bedroom door started to glow bright orange and my heart beat hard. I spun around but the glow was gone. Was it the vodka? Was my imagination freaking out from being in here? My head started to throb and I went back to my laptop. The screen had gone black and I sat down to try and relax with another movie. I pressed the power button. Nothing.

A hard knock against the bedroom door made my knee jerk up and the laptop flew into the air, hitting the wall and landing upside down on the floor. I spun around and saw the door rattling again.

The hell with this.

I grabbed my bag and computer and hurried to the front door. I swung it open and ran onto the road. I sprinted for a good thirty seconds and then stopped and looked back.

The light in the cabin window was like a glowing yellow eye in the night.

I took my cell phone out of my pocket and texted Heather.

Come get me now.

I lowered the phone and stood in the middle of the dark, wet road. The leaves rustled in the wind above me and an owl hooted in the woods. I barely even knew Heather but I hoped she was still up and had her phone by her. I swallowed hard and pulled my overnight bag tight to my body. It sucked giving up like this but I didn't care. That cabin was evil.

I stood there for what felt like an hour but when a set of bright yellow headlights appeared down the road I checked my phone and saw only twenty minutes had gone by.

Heather pulled the Jeep up and I got in.

"Not all that fun, huh?" she asked as I put my seatbelt on.

"No, not really," I said.

My spine chilled as Heather drove up to the cabin. She swung around the parking area in front of it and then hit the accelerator hard enough to throw me back against the seat. We drove in silence as the Jeep's headlights cut through the darkness and lit the dirt road in a yellow glow. Heather made a hard right past a wooden street sign and the yellow lights lit up University Road ahead.

Five minutes later we were driving through campus and I finally felt the weight of the cabin off my back.

"So what really was that place?" I asked.

Heather turned the Jeep onto Mission Street and gave a little nod with her head. "Did you look over those photos?" she asked as she made a quick turn on Gallow; my dorm was straight ahead.

"Yeah, I looked at them all," I said.

"Well, of those three kids, one of them escaped the parents, grew up, and inherited the cabin," she said as she pulled up to my dorm. "She's actually a student at Northern."

I didn't want to ask but I did. "What's her name?" I asked looking straight at Heather.

Heather slowed the Jeep and stopped in front of the dorm. She turned and stared at me. "Take a wild guess."

My eyes widened and she nodded.

The Jeep's engine hummed and I heard some guys laughing about something stupid from the open window of one of the dorm rooms.

"You're kidding," I said.

Heather shook her head.

I popped open the Jeep door, jumped out, and shut it. Heather drove off and I watched the red tail lights disappear into night. I didn't know exactly what was in that cabin's bedroom and I didn't want to. But I was done with Alpha Delta.

And I now knew that no matter how beautiful the area, there were some places you never wanted to stay overnight.

Racing the Ghost

sat in bed and stared at the TV. It was some old sci-fi flick on one of the hotel's movie channels. But I wasn't really watching. My mind raced with images of burning crashed cars and howling race fans and I knew I wasn't going to be able to unwind without a little help tonight. I ran my hands through my hair, got up, and walked over to the bathroom. On the counter next to the little basket of soaps and body gels that every four star chain hotel leaves you was my bottle of Xanax. Mac, our team doctor, had prescribed it to me after the Texas race and I'd been on it for the past two months.

Four races and three first-place finishes later I was still on it.

But Joey's ghost was still visiting me at night.

I walked out of the bathroom and over to the window. The city lights glittered like electric gold medals, but despite my competitive subconscious, winning just didn't mean as much anymore.

Rubbing the back of my neck, I decided to take a quick shower before the Xanax kicked in. I went back into the bathroom, slid off my Nike shorts, and opened the glass door to the shower. Stepping in, I twisted the nozzle and hot water sprayed down on me. It was my fourth shower of the day, but I didn't care —the showers helped me relax. After about ten minutes I got out and caught a quick blue blur of a sharp jawline and a wisp of transparent hair in the steamed mirror.

Looked like Joey was back for the night.

I dried off, slipped my shorts back on, and walked out of the bathroom.

Joey now sat in the chair by the dresser. He might have just been a wispy, wavy version of himself, but it was him. He stared straight ahead like I wasn't even in the room and as I felt the pills start to kick in I climbed back into bed and drifted off to sleep.

The next two weeks were a haze. The final race of the season was in a desert race town outside of Vegas and a win would get the team the open wheels championship for the year. A lot of money was involved and all the leverage I could ever want for getting my new contract next year was at stake.

But my concentration was hit or miss.

The team had pushed Joey—pushed him real hard. He'd gone six seasons as the lead driver without missing a race and he'd brought home three league championships during that time. I'd learned a ton as the number two guy during Joey's reign and when his car had gone up in flames last year I'd gotten the call just a day later to take over his spot—before what was left of Joey had even been buried. It had all been great at first, a big bump in prize money, the women damn near ran each other over to get me at the clubs, and for the first time in my life I felt like a success.

But then the stress of being one bad race away from winding up an ink spot on the race track myself hit.

And that's when I started to get the nightly visits from Joey.

We arrived in Vegas on Monday and I did the time trial on Tuesday. I ran the third fastest time and got the three spot in the poll position. The race was Saturday at 1:00 p.m. and I spent the next few days going over the race plan and hanging out by the pool. Joey didn't visit me the first couple of nights, but around 3:00 a.m. on Friday I opened my eyes and saw him hovering over the foot of the bed staring at me.

Thank God for Xanax.

I shut my eyes and went back to sleep.

My alarm went off at 9:00 a.m. and I showered, got a quick workout in the hotel gym, and then met with the team to go over race stuff. By noon we were at the track and at 12:50 p.m. I was doing the warm-up laps on the race field. The image of Joey floating over my bed popped into my head and a cold sweat broke out on my chest.

When the checkered flag dropped I hit the gas and the car shot up to ninety. A few seconds later I was at 1:30 and I settled in for the long race. The first hundred laps went smooth; I was in fourth which was a good spot for me and I held the position for the next thirty laps. I made my move after that, burning around turn two and passing up the #8 car to move into second place. Another few laps went by and the rest of the field started to fall back. It was just #3 and me. We hit the final lap and he was a single car length ahead of me.

I gripped the wheel tight as the image of Joey's car igniting in flame shot into my mind but I shook it off and floored it. I got the nose of my car to dead even with #8 and then I was ahead. Another two hundred yards and I was there. I glanced up and saw Joey's blank ghost face staring at me in the rearview mirror. My eyes flipped back to the track—clear road ahead, a hundred yards to go. I glanced at the mirror.

Joey was gone.

A second later I shot through the finish line the winner.

I lapped around the course while watching the crowd clap and cheer but for me everything had gone quiet. When I got to the winner's circle my team had bottles of champagne overflowing and were all smiles and hugs. I got out of the car, took off my helmet, and handed it to Sam, our crew chief, and just kept walking.

"Caleb! Where you going?" Sam yelled.

I didn't answer and just kept walking. Past the other drivers, past the crowd, and towards an open gate that would let me exit the track. I walked through the gate and ignored the pats on my back. In the distance, the Nevada mountains rolled against the blue sky and the desert highway stretched in a straight line far past the raceway.

And I just kept walking, never looking back.

On the Run

stumbled out of the car and onto the desert roadside. My upper leg hurt like hell but luckily the bullet had only hit muscle and I'd wrapped it tight enough that the bleeding had stopped. A full moon had risen in the light purple sky and it gave the old church a soft, white glow. Fortunately, the place looked like it'd been abandoned years ago. I pressed the car door shut, limped around the front of the car, and started making my way around the sharp rocks and stubby cacti towards the church.

As I hobbled past a couple of ravens sitting on top of a ten-foot-tall saguaro cactus, the church got watery like a mirage. Fatigue had set in around ten miles back and I guessed the stress of not knowing whether or not I had a bullet inside of me might be causing my sight to blur.

But even then, it wasn't the leg I was really worried about. It was that knife-loving hothead, Vincent. He'd taken a bullet in the gut and I was pretty sure it'd killed him. In all honesty, I hoped it had. He'd been a lousy brother-in-law and had killed for money with that Bowie knife of his on at least three occasions that I knew of.

Something his sister—my wife—Melissa didn't know about.

But I'd still let him bully me into pulling the robbery with him because of the leverage he'd had on me knowing I'd cheated on her a year ago. Of course, she'd left me anyways once she'd discovered our plans to knock off a Kansas bank.

Life sure had a funny sense of humor.

I'd been on the run now for the past two days, but at least I hadn't shot anyone during the robbery—I'd let Vincent do the killing, which he was more than happy to do with his precious knife. As far as the escape plan down to Mexico, I was in good shape. Another day of driving and I'd cross over the border; if Vincent really was six feet under, the law would be mostly satisfied and shouldn't be as hard-charging to find me.

But you never really know, and that's why I had to rest up and keep moving.

I hobbled up to the big double doors of the church and pushed one of them open. The smell of dry wood and dust hit my nostrils and the dim purple light coming through thin rectangular windows in the walls gave just enough light for me to see what was inside. Two rows of six benches, a pew on a stage at the far end, and—thankfully—half-used candles in copper candle holders on shelves attached to the walls.

It'd be fully dark outside in about an hour and this would be as good a place as any to hole up for the night.

I went back outside and looked out at the single stretch of highway that probably went another couple hundred miles before the next town. I took out my Colt and checked the barrel; it was loaded. If somehow Vincent did survive and made it this far there'd be a decent chance he'd stop here too. And that's not at all what I wanted.

I leaned back against the church and just stared out at the desert. After a few minutes I glimpsed a pack of coyotes trotting through the brush and a minute later a rattle snake slithered out of a hole only ten or so feet in front of me.

Time to get back inside.

It was now almost too dark to see inside the church but I could still make out the candles and I walked up to the first and took my book of matches out of my coat pocket. Tearing off a match, I struck it against the rough strip and it lit in orange flame. I held it to the candle and an orange flame jumped off the wick, lighting the church wall in a burnt orange glow. I lit the rest of the candles, took a drink from my water bottle, and lay down on one of the benches. As I watched the candle light flicker over the vaulted ceiling, I thought about Melissa and my eyelids quickly got heavy.

A sharp tapping against the window woke me and I lay there listening to it. It had a metal sound, like the edge of a knife being tapped against the glass. I shut my eyes again.

"*Roberrrr,*" a thin voice hissed in the wind outside the window.

I shot to my feet and my leg burned like someone had poured a pint of whisky on my wound. There was no way I'd heard my name. It was the wind and my tired mind playing tricks on me.

Unless, of course, Vincent had survived and made it here.

No, I'd imagined it. Vincent was history. The whipping wind, the coyote howls, my throbbing leg. It was all getting to me.

But still.

I took the gun out of its holster and went to the door. Lifting the deadbolt I pulled the door open to see nothing but bright stars, desert, and black sky. A gust of wind blew some tumbleweed across the road past my car.

Just my car.

No one had called out my name.

A stronger blast of wind shook the walls of the church and again I heard what sounded like my name hissed around the outside corner of the church. My shoulders tightened but I shook my head.

Just a delusion with my burnt-out mind and this damn desert wind.

And yet ...

I raised the gun and walked back outside towards the corner of the church. The wind whipped faster and faster the closer I got and as I stepped around the corner I held the gun out, ready to shoot.

And of course, nothing was there.

I took a deep breath, lowered the gun, and went back inside the church. It was tempting to get back in the car and drive for the border tonight, but between the wind, the darkness, and my leg, I figured I'd better wait it out. No sense in risking a crash just because I was hearing silly things.

I sat back down and rubbed my chin. It'd been three days since I'd shaved and the stubble brushed against my hand like soft little prickers. This was turning into a long night.

The tapping against the glass started again and my shoulders got tight.

It was heavier this time too, like it might just break through the glass. I looked at the window but all I saw was the black of night. My spine chilled when a scraping sound slid up and down the church door. It moved slowly, like a knife being sharpened—just like Vincent used to do it against that damn flat rock he carried with him.

And I knew there was just no damn way he'd survived that gut shot wound.

I walked up to the door with my Colt out, ready to shoot. Cocking the gun, I wrapped my hand around the door handle and flung the door open.

Again, no one was there.

But I didn't care.

I stepped outside and fired a shot into the air. "Vincent!" I yelled. "It was your fault, Vincent! You got yourself killed, and don't think you're going to be haunting me! You try to and I will find you sister and tell her exactly what you were! You don't have any leverage over me!"

I shut the church door and rubbed my forehead.

I had to get some sleep.

Sitting down against the wall next to the row of candles, I closed my eyes and listened to the now much quieter wind echo through the desert and drifted off to sleep. When I woke up, sunbeams shined through the windows, lighting the church in a golden glow. I pushed myself to my feet, walked to the church door, and opened it up. The sky stretched like a sea of light blue and the car sat at the side of the road just like I'd left it.

And the wind was only a gentle warm breeze.

I stepped outside, pulled the door shut, and walked to the car. It would take about six hours to reach the border and then I'd be home free. My leg still hurt, but my thoughts and vision were clear and I fired up the car and drove off. Maybe I'd try to contact Melissa once I got past the border, but it would be a while. I didn't want to risk anyone finding me.

Although maybe someone already had.

And as I rolled the window down and held my hand out in the already hot morning wind, I hoped there'd be no more Vincent in my life.

But he'd always been a persistent son of a bitch.

And it wouldn't shock me to hear that knife-tappin' son of a bitch again one of these nights.

Ice Skating with a Ghost

gazed out at the frozen lake. Gray sky, a thin sheet of white snow on the lawns of the homes around the lake, and gray ice. The whole thing was like a white-and-gray painting—there was even a patch of gray fog straight ahead close to the shoreline at the other end. It was hard to believe we had something like this right behind our own backyard, but my family had moved away from Florida to Iowa last week and here it was. My skates, which I hadn't worn since last year, were a little tight but they'd be fine for now; I stepped onto the ice. It'd been over a year since I'd finished 5th in the Midwest eleven- to twelve-year-old girls' championship, but skating was sort of like riding a bike and I wanted to start practicing my moves again right away. My knees wobbled a bit as I started to move around but they weren't too bad and I started to skate. As I glided back and forth past the shoreline for a few minutes my legs started to feel stronger and the wobbling went away.

It felt great to be on the ice again, and this would be a great place to practice on my own before I started really getting rating to compete again. I did a little spin and thought about a story I overheard a woman at the market tell my mom about a world-class junior skater who used to skate out here but suddenly died from a sick heart a few years ago. It was a sad story but it made me feel sort of inspired to be using the same ice that someone as good as her did—maybe I'd even figure out how to pull off a perfect double axel like the woman said the girl was known for.

Skating away from the shore, I started to head towards the center of the lake. I wouldn't go past that of course—my mom had told me a bunch of times to stay close to the house—but the lake was big enough where I'd have plenty of room to move by just going part of the way out. As I skated around the ice I looked at the homes that wrapped around the lake. They were big and made of brick like ours and it was probably a couple of miles around the entire lake.

When I got about a hundred yards out, I picked up speed and did a couple of simple figure eights and then started practicing different jumps. After about a half hour I took a break and stared at the north side of the lake. The patch of fog had grown into a sort of cloudy gray wall that stretched maybe fifty feet end to end. I skated backwards while staring at it and my stomach quivered when what looked like a thin, gray arm and leg darted in and out of the darker part of the fog. I stopped and stared. A blurry figure, maybe about five feet tall, spun out of the darker part of the fog. It moved like a girl and I thought I could see wisps of long hair, but I couldn't really see any details about her; it was like watching a thin shadow glide around. I watched as she did a perfect axel and then a toe loop jump and I decided I had to get a closer look at her.

I started to skate towards the fog as the cold air pressed against my face like an invisible ice mask. When I got to around the midway point, the girl did another toe loop and then faded into the thicker part of the fog. I stopped and waited for a couple of minutes but she didn't come back. I shrugged, skated back to shore, put on my skate guards, and went home.

On Wednesday I was back out there again. Soft white flurries fell from the cold sky onto the ice and made a light sheet of snow that I could easily skate through. The fog from the other day was gone and I could now see what looked like a black metal bench at the edge of the lake. I practiced for a while and when I tried to do an axel my ankle gave way on the landing and I fell face first, catching myself with my thick wool mittens before my face could hit the ice. My arms ached a little as I pushed myself up.

I looked back across the lake; the fog was back.

A second later the shadow girl skated through it.

I watched her do a flip and I started to skate towards her again. When I got to the center of the lake she did an axel and faded into the fog. I skated around on my side of the ice, watching the fog for a while, but she never came back.

I didn't get to skate on Thursday or Friday, but Saturday afternoon I was back out there and so was the fog. I waited for a few minutes and when I saw the shadowy girl spin across the fog and do an amazing double axel, my skin tingled and I started again to skate towards her. The wind whipped into my face, making my eyes sting, but I still wobbled forward, holding my hand a little in front of my eyes to block the wind. After a few minutes I crossed the center of the lake and when I brought my hand down the fog had disappeared again.

And so had the shadow girl.

But I kept going.

A moment later I skated into the fog. The wind danced around me like it was trying to spin me in a circle and it got really hard to know which way I was going. I could only see a few feet in front of me but in the corner of my eye I caught a glimpse of a wispy figure twirling in the grayness. When I turned my head, there was nothing there. I called out, "Hello," but my voice sounded like a high-pitched whisper in the wind.

My tired legs trembled and my heart raced. I kept skating though, and a few seconds later the dark frame of the bench appeared. I skated towards it and when I reached the edge of the shore I saw a flat, white stone under the thin layer of snow in front of the bench. There were words etched into the stone. I knelt down and brushed away the snow.

In memory of Michelle Laser, 1998-2010. May she skate forever.

I turned around and the fog was gone. A gust of wind pushed at my side and I balanced myself by bracing my skate into the ice. Looking over the lake I saw what looked like a few kids around my age stepping onto the ice at the far west side. I leaned forward and started to skate towards them.

And even though it was sad knowing the girl had died so young, I'd be back tomorrow to watch Michelle's ghost.

After all, she was the only one I knew who could pull of a perfect double axel.

Late Night Arcade and the Pinball Wizard

:27 a.m. Officially the arcade closed at 1:00 a.m. but I'd let a few of my buddies stick around and finish their air hockey tournament. I didn't mind though. My wild Uncle Sam owned the place and had hired me last week to work the late shift. He'd barely told me anything about the job—Sammy was a gambler and a pretty carefree guy—but it was a sweet gig. Play video games, listen to music, hang out with friends—it beat the hell out of working at the burger joint. In fact, all I really had to do was keep an eye on things, make a note of any games not working right, and close up at night. Easy stuff.

With everyone gone now, I killed the music and started cleaning up the place. Under the red neon lights that ran across the ceiling were six rows of eight games with more games lined up against the wall around them. I grabbed the broom and dustpan from the supply closet and began to sweep up the black, carpeted aisles between the games. As I made my way down the second row my heart jumped when the laser blasts of Star Crashers shot through the arcade. The games stayed on at night but went into a sleep mode where the screens went dark and the sound went off. I set the broom against the racing game, Track Burners, and listened. I was positive everyone was gone, but maybe some kid had snuck in when I was talking with the guys before they left. Rubbing my hands together, I walked over to the middle of the sixth row where Star Crashers was.

The game was on all right, but no one was there.

I pulled the plug out of the floor socket and then went back to my broom. I didn't know much about how these things worked but

I figured it was possible their wiring could get tripped up once in a while and turn them on.

I began sweeping again and the laser blasts started right back up. I ran to the game to see the plug back in and the game going. Somebody was in here and having a good time messing with me. I quickly stepped past the games to the little flight of stairs that led to the manager's booth that overlooked the arcade. Inside was a monitor that recorded all the visual and audio that went on in the place and I could rewind it and see who the little brat was. When I got inside, I stopped and looked through the window at the floor below. I couldn't see anyone and had no idea where anyone could be hiding. It didn't matter though; the monitor would show me what I needed to know. I went up to it and tapped the reverse key on the keyboard. The video started to rewind and I went back a full ten minutes. I hit play and watched.

Nothing happened for the first four minutes, but at the 5:27 mark a high-pitched distorted noise like a record being played in reverse screeched out of the monitor's speakers. Space Crashers' screen flipped on and within the screeching and laser blasts I swore I could hear a kid's voice twisting and turning. Thirty seconds later I showed up and pulled the plug.

Right after I walked away the monitor blacked out.

When it came back a few seconds later the game was going again.

Maybe I just needed some sleep. I shut everything else down and went home.

The next night at 1:07 a.m. it all started again. I went through the same process. Check the game, see no one there, unplug it, game goes back on as soon as I walk away, weird noises on the monitor. The same routine also went down on Wednesday, but on Thursday when I went to the monitor, I slowed the audio down.

"*It's your turrrrn. It's your turrrrn,*" scratched out of the speakers in a voice that sounded like it belonged to a little kid trapped inside some dimension made of static.

Goose bumps popped up on my arms and my back broke out in a cold sweat.

I closed up the arcade and got the hell out of there.

But the next day all I could think about was what I'd heard on monitor.

That night when the game went on, instead of just unplugging it and walking off, I walked right up to it and looked at the screen. It was set on two-player mode and the second player light was blinking. I swallowed hard, pressed the "fire" button, and started playing. For the next five minutes I swerved and spun my ship as I blasted alien attackers and asteroids before a missile blew me up.

The score at the top of the screen showed "Player 1 - 68,314, Player 2 - 62,005."

I stepped back and waited for the game to go to sleep. When it did a few minutes later, I ran to the booth and checked the monitor. I watched myself play and as soon as my game ended I swore I heard a little chuckle come out of the speakers.

Hurrying out of the booth, I closed up the arcade and went home. I had the rest of the weekend off and Sunday night my Uncle Sammy called.

"Hey, Shawn. Haven't had a chance to talk to you this week, but I wanted to know how everything's going at the arcade?"

My mind swam with the image of me playing a video game against an invisible kid from a static dimension. "Everything's good," I said.

"OK, great. So have you met Bobby yet?" Sam asked.

"Um, I don't know," I said.

"Well, he's the ghost kid who comes in after we close. He used to come in all the time and play Space Crashers but he died in a bad car accident about three years ago and his ghost has been coming in around closing time ever since. He's a nice kid; just play a game with him and then he'll go away for the night."

I rubbed my forehead. "OK, yeah, sure, Bobby. No problem," I said.

"All right, great!" Sam said. "Well, keep up the good work and always remember to take the trash out at night. I'll talk to you next week, OK?"

I shook my head and half-smiled. "Sure thing, Sam."

"OK, kid. Be good. Bye."

There was a click and Sam was gone.

The next night Bobby showed up at 1:11 a.m. and we played our game. After we were done the game machine stayed quiet, and I finished cleaning up and left. We then played every night for the rest of the week and then the rest of the month after that.

And I still haven't won a game.

Grandpa's Watch

My time with my grandfather was special, all the more so if it was time spent in the mountains where we would go for walks and he would tell me tales. He taught me how to read poetry, how to tell stories, how to read signs in the wilderness, and just generally filled up my time with him with magic tales of a time far different than my own. I think he enjoyed telling me about his life through his stories and it always felt great when he put his arm around my shoulders as we walked. I learned a thing or two about nature in this vast world of life lessons he made our own.

It was very difficult for me when I heard my grandfather was ill; I'd just thought he was sick and would get better, but I found out that he was dying. I didn't know how to come to terms with that, but when I was told he wanted to see me in the hospital, it finally sunk in and hit me hard. I didn't want to see him that way and have that be my last memory of him. I wanted to remember him as the kind man who took time with me and made part of my life a very precious one. This was the man who taught me a lot of things about life.

I hated hospitals and when I got past all my feelings of what I dreaded in a hospital, I found myself at his door. I didn't want to go in and stood there for a few minutes not wanting to go into his room. When I did finally go in, he was asleep. I was shocked at just how old and frail he looked.

It's been many years since that visit to the hospital—one I'll never forget, nor will I ever forget what happened afterword. He wanted to see me to give me an old pocket watch that he'd had handed down to him from his grandfather. I knew it was old but it looked almost new; they'd all taken very good care of it and I vowed to do the same. He died about a week after my visit and I was hit hard by his death. I just couldn't seem to come to terms with it and all I did was mope around.

About a week after he died I was lying in bed trying to read a book when the watch, which was sitting on my nightstand, clicked open. I was startled but just figured I hadn't closed it properly before and the tension had popped it open. I closed it back up, turned off the light, and went to sleep.

The first thing I did when I woke up every morning was to check out what time it was by looking at the watch he gave me. I always set it in a certain position; it gave me comfort and purpose. I was very exact about it. This morning when I reached for it, it had been moved and was turned over. I just sat looking at it, wondering if I'd done something in the middle of the night I didn't remember. After three nights of the same thing, I figured it wasn't me anymore and it was starting to make me wonder how it was being moved. Each night I went to sleep wondering what would happen. I even took to setting it on certain things, putting books or pencils around it, and even covering it with a washrag one time. It always ended up in the same spot every morning.

Still, I didn't put two and two together. I thought I was being pranked but had no idea who'd do it or why. I tried pretending I was asleep and stayed awake to see who was doing it, but every time I closed my eyes for a moment almost dozing off, when I looked, it was moved. It became so commonplace that after a time I didn't pay much attention to it, which in of itself was rather weird. I should have paid more attention. I also didn't notice specifically when this stopped happening but felt much better about it when it wasn't moving around.

My grandpa always chewed a very fragrant gum, Black Jack if I remember right, and I always loved the smell on him. I think I loved it so much I started smelling it in my room occasionally. I didn't think much of it because it reminded me of better times and I smiled whenever I thought I smelled it. I came home one day after school and found one of my geography books open to a page that my grandfather and I had looked at shortly before he died. It was of the area where he had his cabin and where we used to take our walks. He was teaching me how to read that type of map. I thought this was kind of weird too, but again, I didn't think too much of it—it was just some strange coincidence.

Another time I came home from playing baseball, something my grandpa had loved, when a book on my bed that he'd given to me about pitching opened to the page where he had had me read about throwing a drop. I stood there wondering what was going on; I actually looked around the room for some dumb reason. I knew I wouldn't see anything and think I did it just to buy some time to take this in. I'd been noticing little things that had something to do with my grandfather but in reality, each time it happened it just made me sadder that he was gone.

I even asked my parents if they were playing jokes on me after I told them what had been happening and they just laughed and smiled at me. I went back to my room and my mom followed me, startling me because I didn't know she had.

"Don't tell your dad, but Grandpa always loved you a lot. Maybe he's trying to talk to you."

I looked at my mom like she was crazy and said, "What? Are you kidding? How would he talk to me, he's ..."

She just smiled when I couldn't finish the sentence. After she left I sat down on my bed and thought about it. I couldn't make heads or tails of it and had never believed there was life after death. I don't really know why I didn't—just didn't seem to be something that I'd ever really thought about much. While sitting there thinking, I figured there'd be no harm in at least entertaining the thought that maybe there was life after death and that the ghosts of people could be around, but I was skeptical until I heard a familiar voice in my ear. So real it was like he was sitting right next to me.

I heard, "That's right, son."

I jumped at the voice and waited to hear more. I even asked out loud for him to say something else. After a time I thought maybe I'd heard his voice because I'd been thinking of him and my mind just wanted to hear it again. I didn't know what to think, but I liked the idea of believing there were spirits of past loved ones. For a couple of months nothing else happened and being young, my mind moved on to other things.

The only thing I'd noticed during this time was that whenever I was trying to figure something out, it seemed like his voice in my mind would tell me what to do. I know we all had inner voices and you basically talked to yourself and your intuition would lead you one way or another, but now the voice I heard wasn't mine anymore; it was my grandpa's. I thought it was just me making that happen so I had fun with it and it was actually a comfort.

I had a big test in two days so I was planning to spend my extra time studying in my room. I got everything set up on my desk—all my work to research plus a drink and a few snacks to keep me going. As I sat staring at my work all I could do was think of my grandfather and why he seemed to be on my mind so much. I knew I'd been feeling his presence, but I just thought that was because I missed him so much. What my mom had told me was a nice thought, but did I really believe in ghosts? I kind of sat on the fence on that one and figured I was just making mental adjustments for him being out of my life. It couldn't be any other way. Even if there was such a thing as being a spirit, why would anyone hang around what they'd left? If there was life after, wouldn't there be a better place to go? I was uncertain, but if I dwelled on it too much, I'd never get anything done.

I'd been having strange dreams about my grandfather since he passed, dreams where I was older and we did things that I'd never seen before. Some of the dreams were of things we'd shared but with subtle differences, giving me a strange feeling—almost like he didn't die. I never paid a lot of attention to them because dreams were weird to begin with and I wasn't going to try to make any sense of them. I just knew I felt a little odd the next morning when I woke up, and those were generally the days that something reminded me of my grandfather.

I thought long and hard over the next few years about what I was experiencing and these were just a smattering of all the things that happened. A moved item, suggestions in my head that made me make the correct decision, smelling him in my room, hearing his voice, and at times feeling like he was sitting right next to me. It gave me comfort, but I began to think that I couldn't accept his death and was subconsciously keeping him with me by manifesting these occurrences. I was young and had no experience with matters like this, so it took some time to put it together. He was there with me and making sure I was OK and doing the best things for myself as I grew up. When I made that realization, something else happened that changed my life.

When I accepted that he was with me in spirit as I lay in bed thinking about it, his voice filled my mind again.

"I love you, son. I will always be with you looking after you but it's time to move on and be a man. You don't need my help anymore. Take care of yourself."

This was a lot to take in and at first I thought I'd dreamed it, but when I sat up in bed to collect my thoughts, I no longer felt that he was with me. At least not so obviously as he was before. He was right; I'd done all the right things and was ready to move forward and become the man I am today. Without his help I may not have followed the right roads, even if I did stray a few times, and would not have ended up where I am now—happy and content with a loving family, a fantastic job, and many wonderful friends.

He was no longer there giving me hints and suggestions but I felt him. I felt him in my heart and knew he was around, watching out for me. That gave me comfort and I always smiled when I thought of him and the things we did together. I occasionally talk to him and I feel a warmth that lets me know he's still with me. I will forever treasure the time we had together and look forward to seeing him again.

In the Hospital

I sat against the wall, knees scrunched up and my blankets pulled up around my neck. I couldn't stop shivering even though I wasn't cold … I was terrified. My eyes wouldn't focus and I couldn't take them away from my bedroom door, waiting for it to show up again. I had a feeling this was it, this was the last time, and he was coming for me. I just wish I knew how something like this could happen. Nobody believed me; I didn't believe it myself for a while.

"No, no, no, no! Please! Go away! Go away!" I couldn't believe what was happening. I'd talked to my friends about this and they thought I was crazy. Even my parents didn't believe me.

"What am I going to do?" I mumbled to myself. I could feel that he was almost here and my heart sank; no one would be here to help me. "How could this be happening?"

The temperature dropped and I knew he was close. I couldn't take his torment and cold touches again. I shut my eyes, not wanting to face what I was sure was going to happen.

Crocodile tears started running down my cheeks as I thought I'd never see my family again. I could feel the evil emanating off of it stronger than I ever had before. *Why me?* I thought. *What did I do to deserve this? I never even used to believe in ghosts and now I have one haunting and hurting me?* I wanted to get up and run—wanted to scream as loud as I could—but I couldn't move or talk. All I could do was watch.

I couldn't stop shaking and my tears made it hard to see, but I was thankful for that; I didn't want to watch. Each time he got closer and closer. I didn't know what he wanted, and I didn't think

I'd be able to get away this time. He looked so evil—like he wanted to hurt me or kill me.

I don't know how I knew it because he never talked, but I knew who he was and where he was from. He came from the early nineteenth century and had lived in Boston. His clothes were smelly and he wore a top hat. His name was Charles. And he was an evil son-of-a-bitch; he'd made sure I knew that right off the bat. Seemed like this had been going on all my life and not just the three months it'd been since we moved here. I loved the old house and my room at the back. I loved it because it was so private, but now maybe that wasn't such a good idea.

The first time I had seen him I'd thought I was dreaming. It was just a glimpse of a tall man dressed in old clothes and a top hat. Then I began to see him more often and he would leer at me and come closer. It drove me nuts—he couldn't be real. I didn't believe in this kind of crap ... but then he touched me. It was cold, so cold, but I couldn't do anything to stop him. The last time he visited, I woke up with him lying on top of me; I opened my eyes and his face was right above me. I couldn't move and couldn't breathe and then he kissed me with his dead lips. I can't get the memory of it out of my mind and I knew this day would come.

He was getting close; I could feel the room getting colder as he got closer, just like it had all the other times he came when I was awake. I began to feel faint and I saw movement out of the corner of my eye and as much as I wanted to just fade away, I couldn't. I watched in dreadful fascination as his ugly face floated over to me and I was helpless to even move.

Somebody help me! There was no one who could hear the screaming in my mind. *Oh, God! Oh, God! No! No! No!* He was getting on the bed again, lying down on me with a big grin on his face. *Please, let me die! Don't let him do those things to me again! Please, God, help me!*

"You must come with me, my love."

I knew this was it. I couldn't see anything but him. I tried to move, but he held me still. My muscles were going numb and it was getting harder to breathe. His cold, dead hand was over my mouth and nose and I could feel myself slipping away. I couldn't die like this! I didn't want to be with him in some other … what? What was this? Was I dreaming? *No, it's too real*, I thought. *I know he's here.* I wondered if anyone would know what happened to me after I was gone. *There are no such things as ghosts!* But I knew better. There were, and this one wanted to kill me.

It was peaceful and I started to drift off to sleep. It didn't hurt this time, though, and he began to look familiar, like I'd known him before. Maybe I was supposed to be with him. I wondered what it was like on the other side … I wouldn't have long to wait. My eyelids were getting heavy and I could hardly open them. I started to feel warm—comfortable. *Goodbye everyone, I'll miss you.*

No! I can't! This isn't right! I can't die like this! I had to resist. I had to run. I tried to move again but couldn't. I looked at him and he looked really pissed off and got off me. I had no idea why. I could move and I jumped out of bed and ran to the stairs. Something tripped me and I fell—he got me after all.

My dad found me at the foot of the stairs—one leg broken and barely breathing. The ride to the hospital scared him; it made no sense because he was unwilling to accept the truth. I couldn't blame him; I didn't want to believe it either. He didn't really want to think about it because all he cared about now was getting me some help. I think he held my hand all the way there but I kept slipping in and out of consciousness and I'm not sure.

Waking up, my body felt numb and heavy. I thought I was dead. I didn't want to see and kept my eye closed; I didn't care, nothing mattered anymore. I'd take a look in a moment; there's no hurry.

My dad must have noticed me stirring and said, "Hi, hon, we're here. How do you feel?"

Oh my God! Did he get dad too? I thought. *No, that's not fair!* I heard his voice again sounding like he was far away and I just had to look.

"Dad?"

"Hi, Jess, Mom's here too."

"But … what?"

I saw motion in front of me. The scream came out before I even knew I was screaming. "Please, let me die. Get this over with and quit teasing me!"

"Jessica? I'm Doctor Matthews. You've had quite the bump on the head. How are you feeling?"

I opened my eyes again. My parents were smiling at me and it was a doctor, not him. I must not have actually screamed. He looked so kind. It was so good to see my parents. Was this over? God, I hoped so. Just as I was feeling better, and safe, a cold chill passed by my bed. "No!"

"Jess?"

"Let her sleep. She needs that the most. Her body needs to heal, and sleeping is better than any medicine."

"But she looks afraid!"

"You're right, Mrs. Calader, but she could just be reliving the accident; when she feels better she'll be more aware. She's on a pretty heavy sedative right now. Give her some time."

"Thank you, Doctor."

After the doctor left, my mom and dad walked to the side of my bed and starting talking but I didn't understand a word they said. Both of them rubbed my arm and started to leave. My mom turned and blew me a kiss, at least I think she did but I was so tired and drugged up I don't know if I was dreaming that or what. I don't know why but I tried to fight falling asleep; something was bothering me and I couldn't quite tell what it was. I knew the whole ghost thing was something that made them all look at me funny, but I knew what I had seen—no matter what they said.

As I thought of what had happened, I started to get cold again and it took me a minute to figure out why. He was back! I struggled to fight against the drug and open my eyes. I was shivering and my heart raced a mile a minute but I managed to get one eye halfway opened. I tried to find the call button but my arms didn't work and I waited in terror for his next move. He reached his hand out as he stepped towards me and I felt cold to the bone. Was this it? His hand neared my mouth, but the drugs won and I started to nod off. Just for a split second before I passed out it almost looked like a nurse was taking my temperature. I didn't know what the hell was going on.

I awoke sometime later wondering why he hadn't taken me. The drugs had worn off a bit and the room looked different—stark and bare. Had everything been a dream or had he really been there? I wasn't sure, even as he appeared again at the end of my bed. I gave up and just closed my eyes, wondering what was real or if I was even awake; I couldn't tell anymore. Whatever happened happened … I didn't care. I'd either wake up in the hospital or I'd wake up dead.

My Uncle's Hunting Knife

I was traveling home, alone, from my uncle's funeral. He and I were pretty close since my father had passed some years ago when I was a child and he pretty much raised me. His death was sudden and unexpected and it hit me like a ton of bricks. He'd been my second father and I was the son he'd never had ... he had four daughters and enjoyed teaching me all the "boy" things he couldn't with his daughters. Not that he didn't try; he did—until they found out what boys were and slowly drifted away leaving just me to spend our "boy" time together.

He taught me to hunt and fish and play sports, at least the ones I was interested in; he showed me how to be a man as I grew up. My mother appreciated it since she had my sisters to raise and didn't know quite what to do with me as I grew up. I missed my father terribly, but having my uncle to help me grow up was something special for me. I will always have wonderful memories of him but his passing left a large hole in my heart, and I missed him.

It started on my way home from the funeral; I was so upset that I almost ran off the road. I was driving, lost in my thoughts about my uncle, when out of the corner of my eye I thought I saw a figure. This startled me because I was alone. When I had a second to glance over, I thought I saw my uncle sitting next to me and smiling. I looked back at the road to make sure I was still in my lane and to try and understand seeing what I thought was my uncle but when I looked back, the seat was empty. I felt a weird shiver run through me and got goosebumps and my hands started to shake on the steering wheel. I'd heard about stuff like this but had always thought it was all nonsense. When you died, you died. You didn't go to any place special, you just stopped existing and were absorbed back into the quagmire of the earth. At least that's what I'd grown up believing.

I got home a bit shaken, put my keys on my key hook, and sat down to reflect on what I thought I had seen. After some time I convinced myself that what I'd seen was just me in a place where I missed him so much that my mind made him appear to help me cope with his loss. It was still weird, and I was left feeling a little off. I chalked it up to grief and what your mind does to handle it. I certainly didn't spend much time on it once I came to that conclusion. Ha, little did I know!

The next morning I arose and went into the kitchen to make breakfast. Just as a kind of memorial to my uncle, I decided to make his favorite breakfast, which was one of mine too. I fried up some bacon and then cooked a couple of sunny-side-up eggs in the grease. The toast popped up almost at the same time the eggs. I sat at the table and dug in. As I leaned forward to take a bite, I saw my uncle again. He was sitting directly across from me and as soon as I looked at him, he disappeared. I couldn't take another bite.

I couldn't move and kept staring at the chair I had seen him in. I began to sweat and feel somewhat nauseous so reluctantly, I stood up, went to the sink, and threw some cold water over my face. I felt better, so I headed into the front room and sat in my easy chair, doing nothing, just sitting there and thinking. I wondered if I was obsessing over his death. Maybe I couldn't handle it as well as I thought I did and my subconscious was letting me know I wasn't really doing well with his passing. I could think of no other reasons why I would be seeing him or his ghost. It made me wonder but it also started to spook me. What if ghosts were real? If so, why was he showing up? Was there something he needed to tell me? I had to leave that line of thought or I thought I might lose myself in it. I'd just try to pretend I hadn't seen him.

I watched a movie I had recorded on my DVR the night before and after, feeling pretty good, I went in and got ready for bed. I always read for a bit because it helped me to get to sleep a little quicker. I was lying on my back, reading, when I saw movement out of the corner of my eye and froze in a panic. What the hell was going on? I just knew that if I looked over I would see my uncle again and I couldn't handle that. It didn't matter; I had to look, and sure enough, there he was.

It was weird and frightening to see him in my bed, especially so because what I had originally taken for a smile of pleasure was actually a sad smile; as soon as I realized it and started to look in his eyes, he disappeared again. Suddenly, it seemed like the house decided to make all kinds of noises, which I'm sure it always did, but now it sounded different, almost ominous. My heart raced. I wanted to run but I couldn't move a muscle as I lay there in scared confusion. It seemed like hours before I could finally move again and I jumped out of bed and left the room. I wandered the house without having a clue what I was doing or what I should do. I was now consumed with trying to understand and figure out why I was seeing his spirit. My first thoughts kept bringing me back to my subconscious trying to send me a message.

I never knew I fell asleep, but I woke up on the couch as the sun was rising and I could hear the chitter of birds in my back yard. It was so normal; last night seemed like a dream, and I tried to carry on believing that. It was almost like the feeling of dread you get when you know you might get hit with a football. I sat until the sun had fully risen and my front room was bathed in sunlight. *What do I do now?* I thought. I sighed and started to rise off of the couch and there he was again, sitting in my easy chair. My legs gave out and I fell back on the couch. I shivered in fear and no longer cared why it was happening; I just wanted it to stop.

I looked back over and he was still there. This surprised me because he'd always disappeared when I looked at him. As I watched, he looked like he was trying to tell me something and against my better judgment, I tried to read his lips. I could see that he was struggling and as soon as I thought I was beginning to make out what he was saying, he looked to his left almost fearfully and disappeared. *What am I doing?* I asked myself. *Do I really believe that my uncle is trying to talk to me from the "other side?" I don't believe in that stuff ... do I?* I didn't know anymore and I just sat huddled, feeling very alone.

If there was an afterlife, what did it mean? Do we move on to another place? Do we get to be with those we loved and lost in our lives? I didn't know, but this was sure changing my mind, unless I was really losing touch with reality. I started shivering, shivering so hard my teeth chattered. I had to do something about this one way or the other or I'd go insane.

I felt a little foolish but I decided to call my mom and see what she would say. I could just imagine, and I was sure it wouldn't be good. I got up my nerve and called.

"Hello."

"Hi, Mom. It's me."

"Hi, son, how's things?"

Moms always seemed to know something was going on—must be a mother thing. "I, ah, have to tell you something."

There was a short pause and then she said, "Go ahead."

That was a strange answer for her; she was never that abrupt. "I've been seeing …" I couldn't finish.

She waited and when I didn't continue, to my surprise and horror, she asked, "Your uncle?"

"How … how the hell did you know?"

There was a slight chuckle and she answered, "I've seen him too."

There proceeded to be a long discussion about life and death and what it means, but then she summed it all up by saying, "There's something I think he wanted you to have but I forgot what it was. Maybe he's trying to tell you."

"You have no idea?"

"No. I just know it meant a lot to him for you to have it."

"How do you know?"

"He told me years ago that if he died before me to make sure you got it. I don't think any of us knew he'd go this soon and I've totally forgotten what it was he wanted you to have. I think he knows that and is trying to tell you."

I thought for a moment and had no clue what he could have wanted me to have. I hung up and I saw him again in my sliding glass door. It looked like he was literally *in* the door and now he was shaking his head, looking sad. I stood and watched him, trying to figure out what he wanted me to know. I could see his lips moving but it was unlike any language I knew; I just knew he was trying to talk to me. For a brief second, he looked tired, and then he faded away.

After sleeping on it, I decided to go over to my mom's house to have dinner and see if we could figure out what he could have wanted. I had awoken that morning feeling strange and had dreamed of a hunting knife—nothing else, just the knife. Didn't make much sense, but it was a knife that had been my uncle's. But what the hell was so important about a knife? I remembered it well, but it didn't mean anything special that I knew of.

I went in to my mom's, said hello, and went into her den where we'd put all of his sporting stuff to see if I could feel anything, or find some clue. I felt nothing. As I wondered what in the world he wanted, he appeared again. My mom had just walked in to tell me dinner was ready and I took a quick peek at her.

"Mom. Do you see?"

In a whisper, she answered, "I do."

Before I could say more, he shook his head sadly and faded out. That's the last time I ever saw him, except in my dreams. I never could figure out what he wanted, but I feel like there's a hole in my life because I'll never know. If there's truth to spirits being unhappy, or wandering around in purgatory because something was left undone, it could be happening to him. I never stopped trying to figure it out and someday I hope I get another chance. Maybe it will come to me in my dreams, because living like this hurts. I dream a lot about that knife, but I've never been able to find it; I don't even know for sure if that's what he wanted me to have. I think of him every day of my life.